Mrs MacCready was ever so greedy

by Julie Fulton

Illustrated by Jona Jung

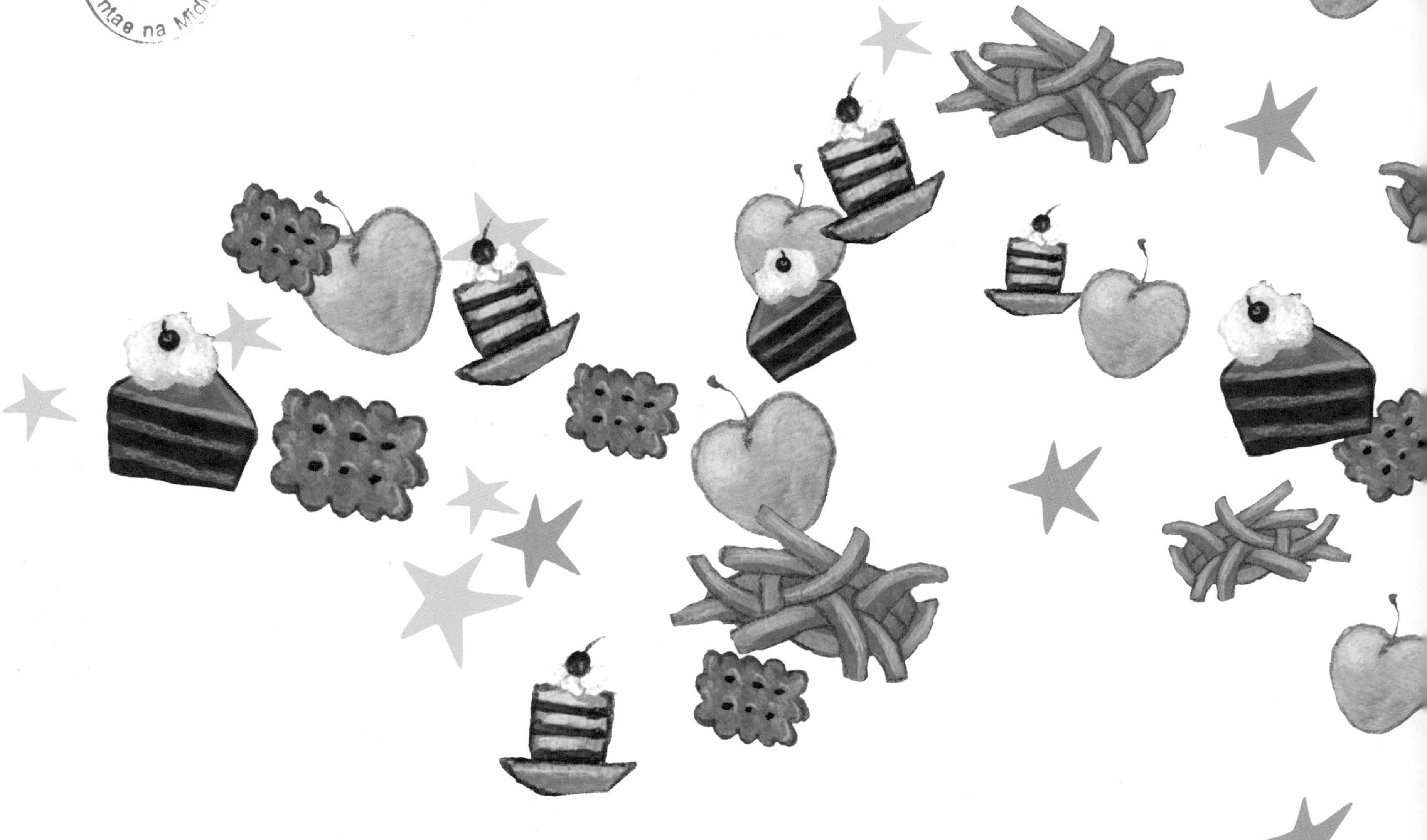

Mrs MacCready was ever so greedy
she did nothing else but **EAT**.
Fish fingers and chips, apples with pips,
plates **FULL** of succulent meat.

Bacon and ham, GOBBLED with jam,
brown eggs scrambled or fried.
All sorts of berries, especially cherries
even with WORMS inside.

An indian curry she ate in a **HURRY**
accompanied by chutney and rice.
A pink wobbly jelly **SLID** down to her belly,
followed by sweet sugar mice.

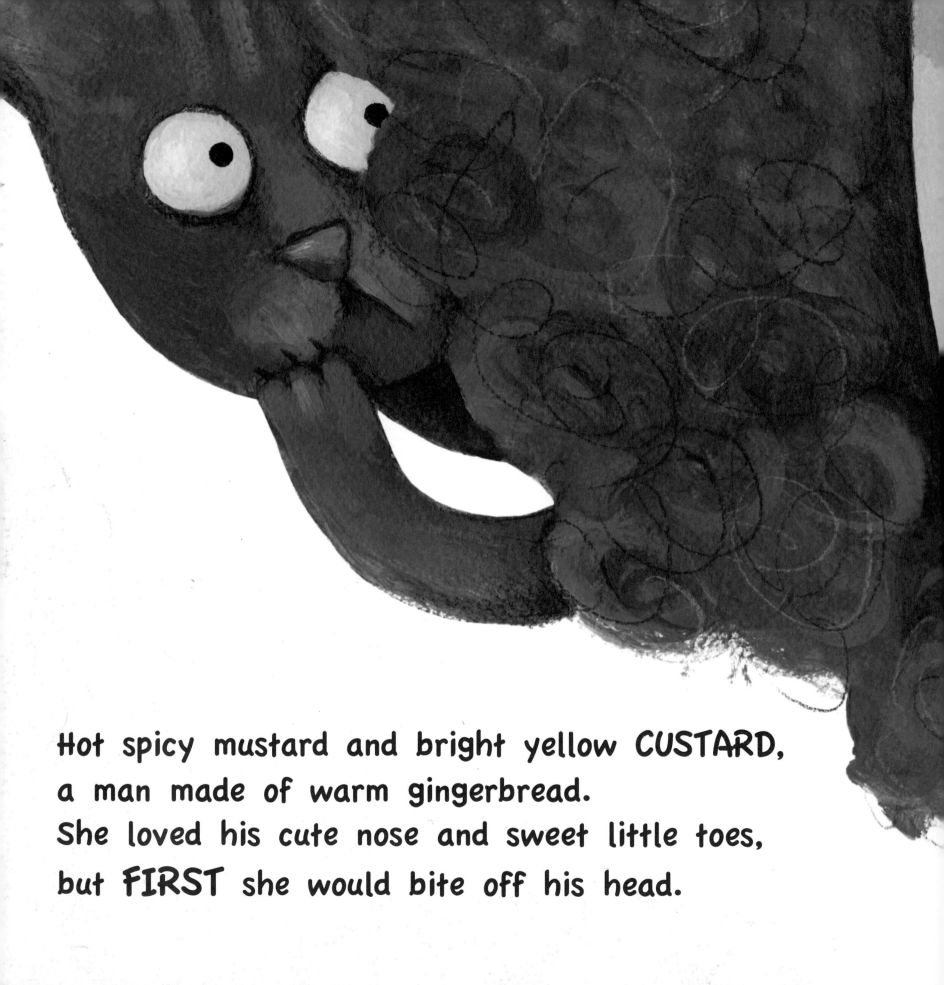

Hot spicy mustard and bright yellow CUSTARD,
a man made of warm gingerbread.
She loved his cute nose and sweet little toes,
but **FIRST** she would bite off his head.

Roast potatoes and pork **PILED** high on her fork
she popped in her mouth to chew,
with **MUSHY** green peas and smelly old cheese
she licked her plate clean, wouldn't you?

When in the right mood her favourite food
was chocolate cake covered in CREAM,
with strawberries on top and a big glass of pop,
it MADE all her neighbours scream.

'Mrs MacCready, you're far too GREEDY,
please find something else to do,
like play in the park or HUNT after dark,
it's really much better for you.'

But Mrs MacCready, ever so GREEDY
and certain that she knew best,
grew bigger and bigger till nothing would fit her
not even her FANCY string vest.

The neighbours they tried to keep her inside,
HIDDEN so no-one could see,
but one day a **PAPER** heard of the caper
and printed the following plea...

...'A rather large lady from Hamilton Shady needs something **NEW** to wear.
It has to be large, the size of a barge.
DO YOU have an item to spare?'

The readers were good and did what they could
sending her all **SORTS** of stuff.
Trousers and shirts, jumpers and skirts,
but **NONE** of it quite **BIG** enough.

A parachute came, far too tight for her frame,
a hot air **BALLOON** was too small.
A wedding marquee decorated for **FREE**
was really just no good at all.

Then a present was sent, a circus tent,
it dropped on the mat with a CLANG,
but it was all too late, meeting her fate
the lady went off with a **BANG!**

Mrs MacCready was ever so greedy
is an original concept by
© Julie Fulton

Author : Julie Fulton

Illustrated by Jona Jung
Jona Jung is represented
by MSM Studio
www.msmstudio.eu

A CIP catalogue record for this book
is available from the British Library.

**PUBLISHED BY MAVERICK ARTS
PUBLISHING LTD**

©Maverick Arts Publishing Limited (2011)

Studio 4,
Hardham Mill Park,
Pulborough,
RH20 1LA
+44(0) 1798 875980

ISBN 978-1-84886-065-0

www.maverickbooks.co.uk